Library of Congress Cataloging-in-Publication Data

Walton, Rick.
   Will you still love me? / written by Rick Walton ; illustrated by
Brad Teare.
    p.   cm.
   Summary: A son poses a number of scenarios to his father and asks
if, in certain circumstances, his father will still love him.
   ISBN 0-87579-582-X
   [1. Love Fiction.   2. Behavior Fiction.   3. Fathers and sons
Fiction.]   I. Teare, Brad, 1956–   ill. II. Title.
[PZ7.W1774Wi   1999]
[E]—dc21   99-28392
                                                      CIP

Printed in Mexico   18961-6509

10 9 8 7 6 5 4 3 2 1

To Alan and Patrick—I will always love you—RW

For my father, Iwan Teare—BT

WILL YOU STILL LOVE ME?

WRITTEN BY
RICK WALTON

ILLUSTRATED BY
BRAD TEARE

SHADOW MOUNTAIN

Will you always love me?

I will always love you.
No matter what you do, I'll still love you.

Will you still love me if I'm playing baseball in the house and throw the ball through the living room window?

If you throw the ball through the window, I'll show you how to carefully pick up broken glass and throw it away, let you help me cover the window space with plastic, take you with me to buy a new window, give you some jobs you can do to earn money to pay for it, and show you how much more fun it is to play baseball outside.

I'll be sorry about the window,
but I will still love you.
I will always love you.

Will you still love me if I get into your clothes and try them all on and accidentally get strawberry jam on all of your shirts?

If I come home from work and find jam on my shirts, I'll show you how the washing machine works, give you some of my old clothes to play with, and talk with you about respecting other people's things.

I'll hope the jam doesn't stain, but I will still love you.
I will always love you.

Will you still love me if I forget to do my homework seven days in a row and my teacher gets mad at me and makes me stay in during recess and calls you in to talk to her?

If your teacher tells me that you haven't done your homework, I'll agree with her that you should do your homework, I'll explain to you that I'm so smart because I did my homework, I'll help you set up a time just for doing homework, and I'll be there to help you if you need it.

I'll expect you to study hard,
but I will still love you.
I will always love you.

Will you still love me if I'm in the car all by myself and I accidentally let up on the emergency brake and the car rolls down the street and over Mrs. Henry's rosebush and into a brick wall?

If you smash the car through Mrs. Henry's rosebush and into a brick wall, I'll scream and panic. Then when I've calmed down, I'll fix up your cuts and bruises, take you to tell Mrs. Henry you're sorry, help you plant a new rosebush and fix the brick wall, and teach you how cars work so you can be safe in them.

I won't let you play in the car again—ever—but I will still love you.
I will always love you.

Will you still love me if I leave all my toys on the living room floor and you come home from work and step on them and fall and break your leg?

If I break my leg because you left your toys all over the floor, I'll hop to the hospital and get my leg put in a cast. Then we'll have a talk about what happens when you don't take care of your things, we'll make a rule about when and where you can play with your toys, and you'll be my special helper who will do things for me that I can't do for myself because my leg is broken.

My leg will hurt, but I will still love you.
I will always love you.

Will you still love me if you and Mom go out for the evening and leave me with a sitter and after you've left, I throw things at her and refuse to do what she says and call her names and when you come home, she's crying and says she never wants to come back again?

If Mom and I come home and find the sitter in tears, I'll let you babysit your little brother and sister, just to see how hard it is. We'll talk about how you made the sitter sad and how mean that was, I'll help you write a letter telling her that you're very sorry, and when she comes again, we'll hope she doesn't bring a baseball bat.

I'll be disappointed in you, but I'll still love you. I will always love you.

Will you still love me if I run through the house and trip over the telephone cord and knock over the living room lamp and break it and pull the telephone down onto the cat and the cat runs into the kitchen and onto the kitchen counter and knocks the china onto the floor where it shatters?

If the house looks like a tornado hit it because you were running, I'll help you clean up the mess and apologize to your mother, we'll comfort the cat, and then before you have dinner, I'll let you make a list of one hundred reasons we shouldn't run in the house.

I'll shake my head and groan,
but I will still love you.
I will always love you.

And now, Son, if I tell you it's your bedtime, and I make you go to bed so that tomorrow you'll have enough energy to go to school and to learn and then to walk home, staying away from brick walls and Mrs. Henry's rosebush,

and when you get home, to do your homework

and then to play baseball—but not in the house or in the car—and then to walk into the house and play with your toys, but not with my clothes and especially not with strawberry jam, and then to put your toys away, while the whole time you're being nice to everyone, even the cat,

will you still love me?

I will still love you. I will always love you.

About the author

RICK WALTON is the author of over thirty-five books for children. His works include joke books, picture books, a collection of poetry, an activity book, and educational software. He loves to read, travel, play the guitar, study foreign languages, and write. Rick was born and raised in Utah, and lives in Provo with his wife and their four children. The things you have read about in this book have actually happened to Rick.

About the illustrator

BRAD TEARE'S illustrations have been published by Random House, Berkley Publishing Group, and the *New York Times*. He most recently illustrated *Dance, Pioneer, Dance!* He lives with his wife and teenaged daughter in Providence, Utah.